A GUIDE'S DAY OFF

PALMETTO
PUBLISHING
Charleston, SC
www.PalmettoPublishing.com

Copyright © 2023 by Jon Lee

All rights reserved

No portion of this book may be reproduced, stored in a retrieval system, or transmitted in any form by any means—electronic, mechanical, photocopy, recording, or other—except for brief quotations in printed reviews, without prior permission of the author.

Paperback ISBN: 979-8-8229-3162-6

A GUIDE'S DAY OFF

Jon Lee

I hope that when you have read something I have written, you are immediately taken there.

*Then, depending on the story you are very happy.
Or not long after, wish you never read the damn thing at all.*

TABLE OF CONTENTS

Wyoming   1

Hex   2

Northern Flats   4

Black Bear   6

Tarpon   9

Like What?   10

Hurricane Ian   12

First Trip   14

Middle Creek   16

Ten Point   18

Everglades   20

Five Good Ones   22

Dads Browning   24

Key West   26

Guide   29

Old Florida   30

About the Author   31

WYOMING

The ranch truck rumbled North on 14 towards Powell.
A small dot on the Wyoming map.
"Do you like geology?" She asked.
"Yes." I replied.
"That plateau is actually a upside down mountain top from the Yellowstone eruption."
I looked over. Her left foot was riding on the dash vent.
Window open.
The hot, dry western air beating on us both.
I looked at her like I looked at the great continental divide just to the West of us and I did not say a word.
How could I?

HEX

He stood in the current looking into the last light of the day.
His client, one of the good ones, is standing next to him.

"Do I start casting as soon as the fish start coming up?"
"You can. Or you can wait for a bigger fish to start rising.
I would wait."

Above them the first Hex labored up and floated down in flight.

"They aren't very graceful huh?"
"You think you'd do any better the first time you tried to fly?"

The Mayflies had been going every night for a week and the Smallmouth were already on the flat.
A few splashy boils from smaller fish demonstrated their youthful impatience.

"When the bugs drop, this place is going to explode."
"This is wild man; how long have you been doing this?"
"Since I was a kid."

The Hex worked down to just above the water and the bass turned the place into a boiling mess.
On the edge of a seam near the deeper part of the tail out was the slow, deliberate rise of a big fish.

"There, on the edge. That's her. Lay it out and then mend."
You could hear the rod in motion. Ticking away through the air as it hits then knocks down the massive insects.
Almost as quickly as it landed the fly was gone. Then eight-teen inches of bass went through the air and the line cleared.
He moved down with the net and watched his client play out the first of the night.
Beaten and in the net, they could see the dark broken bars against the lighter sides.
"Man, that fish is lit up."
"This is fucking insane."
"Yeah, get as many as you'd like."

NORTHERN FLATS

Its name is Wilderness, but it isn't remote.
Maybe because when you are standing there you feel like you are on the edge of what is real and what is not.
The wind kicks up from the water and bites into you. Making it difficult to believe what you are feeling as you look out over a place that resembles the lower Florida Keys.

It's true, if I distort my vision a little it looks like I could be pushing around Ballast Key fourteen hundred miles away.

During the summer the island's shores explode with wildflowers in beautiful contrast to the dense cedar thickets that audibly hum with insect life. This place un-fucked by people. All within sight of one of this country's greatest engineering achievements in the last hundred years.

It is here on this edge, where I feel most like myself.
Where I look out and wonder.
How far does it go?
Then if I go far enough, what will happen?

BLACK BEAR

The gravel bar along the river had that low, grey Alaskan
haze over it.
The bear would eventually cross just like he had done every night
for the past week.
When he did, I'd move in.

In waders and a black rain jacket I would keep low. Moving across, the boar would think it was just another bear in the fading light and haze. When he circled and tried to move downwind, I would get my shot. Waiting there alone, sitting next to a large mangle of timber high water had placed there that spring, I thought.

You're a fucking asshole.
When that bear turns and mows you down you will be dead.
Maybe he will turn and go back the way he came?
Sure….

When I looked up along the edge of the alders there he stood. Hunched up. His back feet almost touched his front ones. Head low.
My hand shook as I reached into the quiver and pulled the arrow out.
I paused as the knock missed the string.

Slow down and breathe.
One thing at a time and follow though.

Almost immediately the bear noticed when I moved. I matched his pace until we were thirty yards apart. Kneeling, I extended my pointer finger forward to keep the arrow from rattling off the wood riser of the bow.

Moving around me, his neck outreached and I could hear the deep breaths draw in and exhale with a snort.
In one motion I raised and drew. Settled into my anchor then released.

The brightly painted arrow shaft and dyed turkey feathers disappeared into the black fur.
The bear dropped then turned with a snarl and a growl.
Running full on in the direction he came until he smashed into the wall of alders.
A moment later I could hear him die just inside the thicket.
The last death moans echoed down the river valley.
After, I heard nothing but the sound of the river behind me.

TARPON

She is ancient big. Emerald and purple and silver.
Floating high in the water on the incoming tide. Just up on the flat near the edge.
The image distorted slightly by the waves.

"You see her? At eleven."
"Jesus!"
"Yeah, you got her. Send it three feet in front and a foot past her then slide."

In a moment frozen in time I can see the line mid-loop against the bright sky.
The dark fly following behind.
The angler leaned over; the rod flexed to the cork.
Then her, she's perfect.

LIKE WHAT?

"They're just like Bone fish, right?"
"No."
"Well, I heard they pull just like Redfish."
"I guess, maybe."
"This is the fly huh? They'll eat this?"
"As long as you make a good cast."

The boat slid slowly across the mud flat close to a weed edge. Speed kills in this game and they hate being run over. Who doesn't?

"Big tail. One O'clock."
"Got It."
"Lay the cast past her head then slide."

She sprung forward and pounced on the fly almost immediately.

"Lift!"

In a wake of water and mud the fish pushed off. The line slicing through the water. The reel losing line then backing as the boat kicked forward with the push pole to keep up.

"Hang on, there isn't shit you can do now."
"Man, that's a big fish!"
"Take it easy on her and don't fuck this up."

The fish close to beaten next to the gunnel you could see the large scales lit up in a gold green.
"Holy shit."
"That's twenty plus man."
"This isn't like a Bone at all!"
"No, more like a carp huh?"

HURRICANE IAN

There was a constant drone of generators, chainsaws, heavy diesel engines and helicopters.

Cliff and Sally shuffled through the glass and twisted tin. Looking at the pieces of their lives that lay on the ground. Discarded like none of it had ever mattered. The reality of a drastically altered future and the fear of the unknown set in.

As Sally turned, I yelled out.
"Are you alright?"
"I'm going to go drink."
Then made her way into the doorless and windowless shell of what was their home.
A home that Cliff and his father built so many years ago.
When he turned toward me, he had tears starting down his face.
"What can I do to help Cliff?"
"I don't know man, where do you even start."
He followed Sally into their home, and I did not see them again until the next day.

FIRST TRIP

A year ago, on the day her husband had run his last trip down the river with me.
Only a couple months into his diagnosis of Leukemia and in the middle of the fight.
She was carrying their second child. Due soon.

The river put out its very best that day and each bass I would net for him he would exclaim.
"Man, is there anything better than this!?"
"No."

Five months after that trip his service was held, and I packed up and left to start my season in the salt.

During the winter she reached out.
"I want to learn how to fly fish."
"Sure. When I get back, we'll go."

When she arrived, the river was in good shape, and I knew where a few fish were.
I pointed the jet upriver and made a short run past the same spots her late husband had fished with me. That we too would hit on the way back down.

I broke down the cast and coached her along the way.
"Straight forward and straight back with a pause in the middle."
She did fine. Eventually being able to work enough line out to allow me to start looking.

When I anchored, I had high hopes. It was a spot where a decent down stream cast and swing up onto some rocks usually found a willing smallmouth.
When the line came tight and the bass jumped, she yelled.
"Holy shit! Now what?"
"Pull like hell. You got this."

When I drove the net into the water and bagged her Smallmouth, I thought of him.
As she smiled for a photo with her first bass on fly, I hoped he'd be pleased.
Then I thought back to all the times I had done the exact same thing for him over the years in that same spot, I missed him very much.

MIDDLE CREEK

It's a small thing. Tumbling past the East gate to Yellowstone. Dropping in elevation the further you push up the pass. Who knows how many times I passed it before making a point to fish it.
It would take the entire season to fish from the confluence of the North Fork to where I thought the head waters started. Each day hiking in to where I last stopped before picking up again.

The fishing changed as I moved in elevation.
At what started with Browns and Whitefish changed to Browns and Rainbows then just Rainbows to Brook Trout and finally at the highest elevation, Cutts.

I had pushed past the high-country meadows where the fishing was spectacular, then made my way into the last bit of timber just below the tree line. Most of it being unfishable because of down trees and boulders. The few plunge pools I did fish, held some of the prettiest Cutts I have ever seen.

Closer now to where I believed the headwaters started was a small canyon with steep unclimbable sides. The water fast, shallow and cold.
A few casts into it I stopped.

My gut twisted up and my heart raced. Breathing rapidly, I fought through the panic and did not take another step.
I looked back in the direction I had come from then ahead in the direction I was going. There was nothing there.
For no real reason other than to I looked up and locked eyes with a lion crouched low on a small outcropping in the canyon above me. Twenty steps away.
The moment we made eye contact it turned and in a single bound cleared the rim and was gone.
The one and only cat I have seen in the wild. Although I am certain not the first time one has seen me.
I hung the rod up and hiked in. Eventually finding where the water flowed directly out of the mountain side with such force it was deafening. I took a long drink; the water was so cold it hurt going down. I sat and rested before filling my water bottle and starting the hike out.

TEN POINT

Photo credit: Eric Shaeffer

    I started the long walk back to a place I know well. On the farm where I learned how to bow hunt. But not the place that made me the bow hunter I am now.
    That came later, in a different Mid-Western state.

    A front would push through as the evening went on. Behind me I heard the distinct sound of trees being hit by antlers. I reached for my bow and waited. Out stepped a younger buck, then he walked underneath my stand then began hitting my cover trees. The limbs violently hit me in the tree above.

Off to my right another buck started raking trees. What stepped out was a heavy, fully grown animal.
He pushed off the younger deer and began hitting the same trees. Again, hitting me in my stand.
The younger buck started hitting a ground scrape twenty yards away and this pulled the older buck out from under me.
With a slight posture he pushed the younger deer down the hillside and began hitting the same scrape.
I raised my bow a drew when he pivoted to hit the branches above.

My arrow hit hard, and he was gone. Sixty yards away in less than a minute he lay dead.
In his antlers hung pieces of the trees he had hit. He was dark and heavy.
I knelt down and reached out to make him real. Instantly I was filled with a sense of remorse, elation and relief.
On the place where I learned how to bow hunt.

EVERGLADES

The skiff pounded across Whitewater Bay. Cutting a line of prop wash through the heart of the Everglades.
Past miles of old growth mangroves and creeks mouths we powered down and looked out over the bow at Tarpon Bay.

On the chart its fingers reach inland. Desperate looking. Willing to take any fresh, clean water flowing South. The driving life force not just to Tarpon Bay but the entire Everglades ecosystem.
A diminishing thing that has long been under threat.

It would take seasons to know this place and lifetimes to begin to intimately know the Glades.

The room for opportunity seemed limitless as
I climbed up to the platform and began looking. Trying to find
what we came for, Snook.

In a steady cadence of push and cast, push and cast we hunted.
Near a point the angler took the shot. The fly landed well and one
of the mangrove roots moved.
When it turned, it gave up its side. I could see the long black line
through the water's distortion.

"Big Snook! Slide, slide, slide….Touch it! Hit Her!"

The Snook exploded and went for the trees. The angler low,
leaned back, putting everything he could to her.
"Keep the rod low and fucking pull!"
The water boiled next to the mangroves as the Snook tried to dig
in.
I kicked the skiff off the line and as the pressure built, she turned
and went for deeper water.
"We're good. Now play her out."

Next to the skiff beaten, we landed our first Snook.
As I sent it back, we watched the gold sides and dark back fade
into the Everglades.
I believe we got lucky to leave with a small piece of that place and
those memories are ours.

FIVE GOOD ONES

We ran back into one of my favorite spots. A place no skiff would go let alone a T-top. Through a fifteen-mile maze of mangroves full of Snook and small Tarpon.

I climbed up and settled onto the platform. My client for the day took the bow and peeled enough line off the reel for a cast.
I learned a long time ago to quit asking people about their abilities when they book.
I am better going into it expecting the worst.

"In this mangrove game when you're close you're still a foot away. Now, send it up and let me see what you got."

He then sent a beautiful forty-five-footer that laid out exactly where he wanted. It was slow and deliberate and damn nice. I'd take five good casts in thirty minutes over a hundred shitty ones any day.

For the next few hours, I watched as he threaded those trees and roped snook out. At the end of one of the mangrove lines I hopped down.

"Let me get a new bite guard tied on and get you a new fly. Then we'll push farther back."
"Sounds good."
"You're doing great. Honestly you need a guide like you need another hole in your head."
"I'm not paying you to find me fish."
"No?"
"No, I'm paying you to get me back out of here at the end of the day because I am fucking lost!"
"Keep up the good work and I won't make this a one-way guided trip."
"I can't tell if you're joking."
"Most people can't."

DADS BROWNING

I stood overlooking the city. The city he served and the city I work in.
It was late October. Still and warm. The late evening sun glinting through the trees seemed to set the place on fire.
It was a little past five when I called the nurse in.

In a moment it seemed like a weight had been removed from my shoulders and placed at my feet.
It had been a long road. So, expected.
Still, I left the hospital like I was walking through wet concrete.
I continued into the work ahead. Making sure I did what he asked me to do.
I curbed the grieving knowing I would make time.
After the arrangements were made, the service ended, and I was away from the people I cared little for.

By now the withered corn stalks stood in defiance against the low, grey November sky.
Teek, the old lab kept a steady working pace on the downwind edges.
Dad would have approved.
Going down a hillside we cut in hard. In an explosion of iridescent purple and brown and white a rooster flushed and set.
I shouldered my father's old A5 and swung into a good lead.
The light twelve barked and bit into my shoulder ending the pursuit he loved so much.
Out from the cover Teek broke through holding dad's favorite gamebird.
The long, barred tail feathers dragged through the grass.
One wing covering part of his head.
I thought then how dad would have been pleased.
Then, how much I missed him.

KEY WEST

We both reached a point in our professional lives where time
wasn't going to just appear.
So, we planned the day off.
The only difference between a guide's day on and a guide's day off
is the removal of all expectations.

Now, if you're going to go fuck off with Bear for a day out of Key West, you will be looking for Permit.
Working the channel edges just to the West we found them.
Their dishonesty being legendary.
Poling the skiff down the edge, toward a point we started seeing life.
A small Bonnet working back and forth. Rays hoovering around then a Lemon shark with a serious disposition.

Bear saw them first. A group of five Bones close.
They were milling around, happy. Tails up and bright.
Their mouths moving, feeling the bottom.
All uniform in size.

"Give me a kick!"
With the pole I swung the stern in and kicked the bow away opening up a shot.
Bear laid it out perfectly. Rod low with short slides.
One of the bones broke off the group and charged forward cleaning the shrimp fly off the bottom.
The line cleared off the deck and I poled with everything I had to stay close.
"That's a real Bone!"
"Yes."

With the Bone fish alongside and beaten next to the skiff we hopped in. Bear holding onto a small part of this natural world that plays a major role in his life.

"Eight-Nine pounds?"

"Yeah, every bit of that man."
We then chased the sun back along the powerlines to Lower Sugarloaf Key and loaded up the skiff against a sunset no one could possibly describe.
So, I won't try.

GUIDE

Photo credit: Eric Shaeffer

I am limited only to the amount of fuel I can carry, the length of the river and my stamina to drive a push pole through the heart of the earth.
This life dictated by wind and tide and flows.
Each one pointing me in the direction I will go that day.

I can see and feel every mile in my hands.
I own every push from the back of the skiff and every sweep of the sticks in current from the middle seat.
They are mine and no one else and that cost has reached far past my gunnels.
Regardless of what I have paid, it has been worth it.

OLD FLORIDA

I have heard it quietly pass around in conversation.
If you are one of the people that know, then you are always looking.
Looking for a place in a moment that takes you back there.
But it's not the same.
It's a trick of the mind and a distorted reflection of a time past.

That place is gone and no matter how far you push towards the edge, you'll never find it.

So, in conversation I will hear it and wonder what that must have been like.
Because I have never seen it.

ABOUT THE AUTHOR

Looking for something I haven't found.

www.ingramcontent.com/pod-product-compliance
Lightning Source LLC
LaVergne TN
LVHW061049070526
838201LV00074B/5236